THE MYSTERY AT

DOLPHIN COVE

by Carole Marsh

Published by Gallopade International/Carole Marsh Books.
Printed in the United States of America.

First Edition ©2014 Carole Marsh/Gallopade International/Peachtree City, GA
Current Edition ©February 2015
Ebook edition ©2014
All rights reserved.
Manufactured in Peachtree City, GA

Managing Editor: Janice Baker
Assistant Editor: Sherri Smith Brown
Cover and Content Design: John Hanson

Gallopade is proud to be a member and supporter of these educational organizations and associations:

American Booksellers Association
American Library Association
International Reading Association
National Association for Gifted Children
The National School Supply and Equipment Association
Museum Store Association
Association of Partners for Public Lands
Association of Booksellers for Children

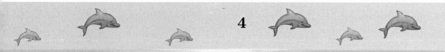

Once upon a time …

Hmm, kids keep asking me to write a mystery book. What shall I do?

Papa said …

Why don't you set the stories in real locations?

That's a great idea! And if I do that, I might as well choose real kids as characters in the stories! But which kids would I pick?

MIMI, PICK ME, PICK ME!

Christina

ME TOO, MIMI, PICK ME, TOO!

Grant

MIMI, ME TOO!

Ella

PAPA, TELL MIMI TO PICK ME!

Avery

MIMI, DON'T FORGET ME!

Evan

Pick me!

You sure are characters, that's all I've got to say!

Yes, you are! And, of course, I choose you! But what should I write about?

National Parks!

SCARY PLACES!

Famous Places!

FUN PLACES!

Disney World!

New York City!

Dracula's Castle

GRAND CANYON

Write one about spiders!

We can go on the *Mystery Girl* airplane ...

I can FLY US anyWHeRe!

Or aboard the *Mimi!*

Take me to the Forbidden City!

Or by surfboard, rickshaw, motorbike, camel ...!

I can put a lot of **history, MYSTERY, science,** legend, lore, and **laughs** in the books! It will be educational and fun!

Good stuff!

And so, join Mimi, Papa, Christina, Grant, Avery, Ella, Evan, and Sadie aboard the *Mystery Girl*—where the adventure is real and so are the characters!

START YOUR ADVENTURE TODAY!

www.carolemarshmysteries.com

A Note from the Author

DELIGHTFUL DOLPHINS

From the time I was a little girl in Atlanta, Georgia, I loved dolphins! No, I never saw any dolphins in Atlanta; we did not have the lovely Georgia Aquarium back then. But my family and I often visited the Georgia and Florida beaches. Off Tybee Island, near Savannah, Georgia, I could easily spy dolphins frolicking in the waves. In Florida, we would go to Marineland—a wonderful attraction where you could see dolphin shows that just seemed magical to me!

I loved to read any book—fiction or non-fiction—that featured dolphins. I have never actually gone swimming with dolphins (riding on the back of one is what I wanted to do!), but once—as an adult, in Emerald Isle, North Carolina, where I lived—a big batch of dolphins came so close to the shore early one morning that they tickled my ankles as I was walking in the waves!

I hope you enjoy learning about dolphins as you dive into my latest mystery! Those beautiful creatures always put a smile on my face!

— *Carole Marsh*

Evan is ready to go fishing!

1

DOLPHIN TRAIN

Avery shoved her long blond hair behind her ears and arched her head back. She closed her eyes lazily, and let the sun shine on her face.

"Now, this is what I call a great first week of summer vacation," she said with a yawn.

"It sure is," agreed her younger sister Ella, gazing across the wide May River gently rolling past them.

Dressed in blue denim shorts and t-shirts, the girls perched on the end of a boat dock, its planks gray and worn from years of scorching sunshine and pounding storms. Their bare feet dangled over the edge. The rippling waves of a rising tide tickled their toes.

White sandbars glistened in the hot sun. Islands of tall, chartreuse **marsh** grass dotted the water. Palmetto trees swayed in the warm breeze.

"Look!" said Ella, pointing. Avery opened one eye to see an osprey swoop down to pluck a fish from the rippling water before soaring back up into the cloudless blue sky.

"I'm so glad Mimi and Papa moved here," said Avery, as her open eyelid fluttered shut.

The tall bluffs of Palmetto Bluff, South Carolina, rose up behind them. The girls, along with their mother, father, younger brother Evan, and baby Sadie, were visiting Mimi and Papa, their grandparents. Their cousin Christina had driven from Savannah to spend a few days with the family, too. Christina attended the Savannah School of Art and Design, known as SCAD.

The kids always had fun with Mimi and Papa. Mimi wrote children's mysteries. She and Papa traveled the world as she researched facts for her books. Avery, Ella, and Evan often got to tag along with their grandparents to **intriguing** new places.

Mimi said their new home in Palmetto Bluff was giving her **inspiration** for lots of new mysteries. And right now, dressed in a scarlet swimsuit and big floppy hat, Mimi sat in the bow of Papa's boat, the *Mimi*, tapping away on her laptop.

Suddenly, Evan, who was perched nearby on the dock, yanked his fishing line from the water.

"ARRRGGGGHH!" he screamed, "something keeps stealing my bait!"

Startled, Avery jumped. "Evan!" she yelled, her eyes flying open. "You scared me to death!"

Just then, a huge gray blur of fish and fin flashed in the water beneath Ella's toes.

"Yikes!" screamed Ella, scrambling to her feet. "It's a shark!" Stumbling and losing her balance, she tumbled into the murky river water.

"That's a dolphin!" yelled Avery, catching a glimpse of the intruder. She ignored her sister splashing in the water. "Look at it go!"

Christina threw down her book and sprang from her seat on the dock. Grabbing her binoculars, she peered at the dolphin quickly gliding away. "Cool! It IS a dolphin!" She extended her hand to help a spewing and sputtering Ella climb up the dock ladder. Soppy wet strands of long blond hair clung to Ella's face. Blades of marsh grass stuck like leeches to her pink t-shirt.

"What's the **commotion**?" hollered Papa, scrambling from the cabin of the *Mimi*. "Is everyone OK?"

"You missed it, Papa," said Evan, his sky-blue eyes twinkling with excitement. "We saw a dolphin, and Ella thought she was shark bait!"

"Ella just swam with a dolphin, so to speak," Christina added. She pulled a green-and-white striped towel from her beach bag and tossed it to her little cousin.

"Look!" shouted Ella. She pointed across the river. "What's that?"

In the distance, a graceful dolphin leaped out of the water and dove back in just as another popped up.

"There's a sister dolphin," Christina said, "or maybe a mama."

"I think there are four!" shouted Ella, as the dolphins swam steadily in a straight line down the river.

"It's like a dolphin train!" Avery exclaimed.

"Papa, what's that creepy old boat following them?" asked Ella.

"It looks like an old fishing boat or kind of like a shrimp boat, but different," said Papa. He pushed his black cowboy hat back off his forehead and squinted at the boat in the distance. "See? It has booms out to the side with nets hanging on them."

"It looks like a ghost boat, Captain," said Evan, saluting his grandpa.

"It looks to me like it's going to run right over those dolphins," said Avery worriedly.

"I would love to see a dolphin close up," Ella added, her eyes still glued to the animals as they disappeared from view.

"You just did, Ella!" yelled Evan, giggling as he hurled his fishing line back into the water.

"Yes, but I thought it was a shark!" replied Ella. "I was scared. I didn't enjoy it. There's a difference."

"Do you want to see one of my favorite things?" Christina asked the girls. She held out a delicate, silver chain from around her neck. "This is my dolphin necklace. I wear it all the time."

"Oooooh! It's beautiful!" Ella said.

The silver dolphin, decorated with blue gemstones and a darker blue eye, sparkled in the sun.

"A lot of **symbolism** surrounds dolphins," said Christina.

"What do you mean?" asked Ella.

"Dolphins represent playfulness, gentleness, happiness, and balance," replied Christina. "Lots of people believe dolphins work together to bring harmony and peace to the ocean.

"In ancient Greece," she continued, "the dolphin represented Apollo, the sun god, Artemis, the moon goddess, and Aphrodite, the goddess of love. Greek legend says that dolphins were responsible for carrying souls of the dead to the Islands of the Blessed."

Evan's head snapped around. "That's spooky!" he said.

"I think it's beautiful," Christina disagreed.

"We need to learn more about dolphins," said Ella.

"Let's make this 'The Summer of the Dolphin,'" Avery added.

"I'm in!" said Evan.

Suddenly, something tugged hard on Evan's fishing line. "WHOA!" he yelled.

SPLASH! Evan tumbled into the waist-high river water. Christina ran to him as he waved his scrawny arms and shook water from his stick-straight blond hair. "OK, I'll pull you up, too," she grumbled and tugged her cousin back onto the dock.

"Fish and bait are now in Davy Jones' Locker!" said Papa with a laugh.

"You're IN, all right!" shouted Ella. Everyone laughed as Ella grabbed her iPod from her backpack and took a selfie of the soaked, smiling duo—she and her brother.

Avery scanned the river. She could no longer see the dolphins, but could still make out the boat following them. She frowned, deep in thought.

Mimi, who hadn't said a word during all the **hoopla**, observed Avery's concerned face and typed: *A ghost ship appeared on the horizon... and the summer would never be the same....*

2

A PIG IN A GHOST BOAT

The kids were lined up, like birds on a telephone wire, on the thick rope hammock that hung between two **gnarled** live oak trees. They **devoured** the turkey and cheese sandwiches that Mimi made for lunch.

Evan licked his fingers. "Mimi makes a gooood sandwich," he said. "But I could've used a little more mayo on mine!" He licked creamy mayonnaise from his fingers and wiped them on his red plaid swim trunks.

"You do like a little turkey and cheese with your mayo, don't you?" said Ella.

Christina munched on a chunky chocolate chip cookie as she read her book. She was happy to spend a few days with her cousins at Mimi and Papa's house before going back to SCAD for summer classes. She loved the **Lowcountry** landscape and the peacefulness of the coast.

"Check out this illustration of things that grow under a pier," said Christina. She held up her book, *Tideland Treasures*. "Here are acorn barnacles, mussels, a starfish, an **anemone**, a finger sponge, a blue crab, and sea pork!"

"Sea pork," chortled Evan. He dashed over to the dock, waded into the marsh muck, and peered beneath the dock. "I don't see any pigs under here!"

The girls giggled. Evan scampered back to the hammock. He beamed. He loved to make the girls laugh. He didn't even have to work that hard to do it.

"I've been thinking," Evan said as he climbed back into the hammock. "Are you sure that wasn't a purpose that almost ate Ella? We drew pictures of purposes in school last year."

"Do you mean a *porpoise*?" asked Christina, grabbing onto the swaying hammock.

"Ba-Bam!" shouted Evan, swinging the hammock harder. "That's what I mean!"

"I know there are lots of dolphins in this river," said Christina, "and all along the Atlantic Coast. But I don't really know how to explain the difference between a dolphin and a porpoise."

"Search it up, Avery," Evan ordered in his best professor voice.

Avery reached into her green paisley backpack and pulled out her iPhone. "What's the difference between a dolphin and a porpoise?" she asked the phone's personal assistant program. Immediately, a browser page popped up.

"Dolphins and porpoises are marine mammals and closely related to whales," Avery read aloud. "Both are extremely intelligent. Dolphins are generally longer and leaner than porpoises. Dolphins have a curved dorsal fin. Porpoises have a triangular fin, somewhat like a shark's fin. Dolphins have bigger mouths and longer snouts than porpoises. Dolphins are very social and less fearful of humans. Porpoises are shy."

"So dolphins probably like a good party, and porpoises would rather stay home and watch TV," Evan said.

Ella giggled. "Let's go to the sandbar," she said. "Maybe we'll see some more dolphins!"

"And maybe we'll see the *ghost boat*," Evan said, trying to sound spooky.

The kids sprang out of the hammock. It was still swinging madly when they grabbed their paddle boards and stepped into the river.

"Hey, Papa!" Christina yelled. "We're going to the sandbar. Ella wants to look for more dolphins."

The kids paddled away from the dock. Papa waved from the *Mimi*. They heard his deep voice singing, "Shrimp boats is a-comin'...their sails are in sight, shrimp boats is a-comin...there's dancin' tonight..."

Avery stood on her orange board and paddled slowly. *"Shrimp boats is a-comin',"* she sang in her head. *"Ghost boats is a-comin'..." That's creepy,* she thought. Then she thought about the dolphins gliding down the river in front of the old boat. *Maybe we will see the dolphins again! After all, THIS is "The Summer of the Dolphin"!*

3

FIDDLER CRABS AND MUCK

Disappointed, the girls trudged along the edges of the marshy river back to Mimi's house. They had paddle-boarded to the sandbars and back, but didn't see one sign of dolphins.

They slogged through the pluff mud, the Lowcountry name for the black, icky mud in which the marsh grass grew.

Pluff! Pluff! Their flip-flops smacked each time they came up out of the gray muck.

"I know why they call it pluff mud," said Avery. "Listen to the sound of our flip-flops!"

"You know this stuff is made of decaying plants and animals," said Christina.

"Yuck!" said Ella.

Pluff! Pluff! Pluff!

"Little marsh creatures make their home in this mud," said Christina. "They feed, breed, and die here."

"Double yuck!" said Ella.

"What kind of little animals do you mean?" asked Avery.

"Oysters, snails, and fiddler crabs," replied Christina.

"I'm a muck monster!" cried Evan, charging up behind them.

The girls stopped to gape at Evan. Black, slimy mud covered his bony legs, ankles, and feet.

"Yooooou stink!" cried Ella, holding her nose.

"I like it," said Evan with a deep inhale.

"You smell like rotten eggs!" said Ella.

"Actually, this whole place smells like rotten eggs," said Avery. "Rotten eggs mixed with salt water. Christina, do you know why it smells so bad?"

Christina pointed toward the river. "Every time the tide comes in," she replied, "it floods the marsh with seawater.

The waterlogged ground is packed with **decomposing** plant and animal material so there's very little oxygen in it."

"Not those yucky marsh creatures again!" said Ella.

"The lack of oxygen," Christina added, "promotes the growth of bacteria which produce the rotten egg smell. And that's why salt marshes smell like rotten eggs."

"Your smell is just way more potent, Evan!" declared Avery.

"What's a potent?" Evan asked.

"It means you smell a lot stronger than normal rotten eggs!" replied Avery.

"Mimi's not going to let you in the house like that," said Christina.

"Oh, she won't mind a little river muck," Evan said cheerfully.

"Look at all the little fiddler crabs!" said Avery, stooping down to inspect them scurrying across the mud.

"Why are they called fiddler crabs?" asked Ella.

"It's because the male has a large reddish front claw that he holds like a fiddle,"

said Christina, bending down. "See? Here's one! Then the opposite smaller claw looks like a bow."

"Why are they waving their fiddle claws?" asked Evan. He bent down to pick one up. "Ouch! He bit me!" Evan shook the fiddler crab off his fingers.

"They're waving to the female fiddler crabs," said Christina. "They're all trying to get girlfriends!"

"Gross!" said Evan. He started counting the crabs. "Look! There are ten fiddlers right here!"

"That's about a square foot," said Christina. "So if you used that measurement of ten fiddlers per square foot, about how many fiddler crabs could be between here and Ella? She's standing about ten feet away."

"Ten times ten is 100," said Avery, who was an excellent math student.

"Are you saying there are about 100 fiddlers between me and Ella?" Evan asked. "That means there must be a million between here and Mimi's house! What if I step on one?" He began to tiptoe carefully around the crabs.

Pluff! Pluff! Pluff! The girls continued their march through the mud.

"I wish there were a hundred dolphins around," said Avery. "I want to get closer to them. I want to be as close as that old fishing boat we saw."

"Let's take a kayak trip out into the river tomorrow and look for dolphins," said Christina. "Papa has a friend who works as a guide to the area. He could take us. That would be a fun trip before I head back to Savannah tomorrow night."

"Maybe I'll jump out of the boat and swim with the dolphins!" said Ella.

"You can't do that, Ella!" said Avery. "It's way too dangerous to swim with wild animals!"

"Aren't Mimi and Papa taking you to Florida when I go back to school?" asked Christina. "I've heard you can go to places there where trained people will teach you how to swim with dolphins."

"I'll look it up," said Avery, sliding her iPhone out of her pocket. "Wow, there are lots of places in Florida to swim with the

dolphins," she exclaimed. "There's one in the Florida Keys, and one at Dolphin World, and one at SeaWorld, and one at Marineland... we'll have to tell Mimi!"

"She'll probably go swimming with the dolphins with us," said Ella. She tried to leap up to make a high-five gesture with Evan— until one of her pink flip-flops stuck in the mud. "Ugh," she said, muck oozing between her toes.

"I'm cold," said Evan, hugging his boney body with his skinny arms. "I forgot my jacket."

"The sun is going down," said Avery. "It always gets cooler when that happens."

"Why?" asked Evan. "That's not fair!"

"I know why," Ella said. "It's because the sun warms the Earth. So when the sun goes down, it gets cooler." She stood on one leg and swished her muddy foot back and forth in the river water.

"Ba-Bam!" said Evan. "I get it!"

"Sorry I can't give this to you, Evan," said Christina as she pulled a lemon-yellow SCAD sweatshirt from her backpack. "You are too mucky! AND you smell bad!" She tugged the sweatshirt over her head. Avery reached up to help Christina untangle her chestnut brown hair from the hood.

"We better scoot or we'll be late for dinner!" said Christina. "Mimi's cooking!"

"Oh, man!" moaned Evan. "You know what that means?"

"Salad!" said the girls.

"Yes, salad!" said Evan, stomping off down the beach.

Avery stuffed her iPhone in her pocket and sighed. Ella wasn't the only one who wanted to swim with the dolphins. She secretly wished she could, too!

4

LOST

Christina, Avery, Ella, and Evan prowled slowly with their heads down. Their eyes darted over every fiddler crab and tiny piece of shell. They were retracing their steps from Mimi's house back to the dock.

"I can't believe I lost my dolphin necklace," said Christina tearfully. "We'll never find it. This is a lost cause. The tide probably carried it away."

"Why would a tide want your necklace?" asked Evan, jerking up his head and staring at Christina. "What is a tide, anyway?"

Christina explained how tides are produced by the moon and sun's **gravitational pull** on the world's oceans. At the beach, the waves come in higher when the tide comes in and lower when the tide goes out.

"Here, in the marshes," said Christina, "there aren't any waves. Instead, the water rises when the tide comes in and covers the grasses. It sweeps in and churns up that bottom muck you like so much, Evan. It brings in fish and tiny organisms to feed and reproduce in the marsh."

"What happens when the tide goes out?" asked Ella.

"It carries away everything—nutrients, live and decaying marsh grass, and other live and dead plants and animals," replied Christina. "It all becomes part of the ocean's **food chain**. The problem is, the tide probably carried away my necklace, too!"

"We'll find it," assured Avery, wrapping her cousin in a hug.

"Look at that spooky boat over there," said Ella, pointing to a **dilapidated** fishing boat tied to a rotten post near the water. *Dolphin Catcher* was painted in faded blue block letters on its bow. Huge, thick, muddy nets hung over its sides. It creaked as it bobbled on the water.

"It looks deserted," said Avery.

"Like a real ghost ship!" said Evan.

"I wonder if a 'dolphin catcher' is anything like a 'dream catcher,'" said Ella. "Remember that dream catcher you made me with the feathers and beads, Christina? Maybe I could have a dream about finding your necklace, and then catch my dream with the dream catcher."

Christina hugged Ella. "Thank you, sweetie. I don't think we have much chance of finding it."

"Well, I think the odds are 50-50," said Avery.

"What's that mean?" asked Evan.

"Odds," said Avery, "are the ratio of the **probability** of something happening to the probability that something will not happen!"

Evan looked confused. "Huh?"

"As far as my necklace goes, we only have two options," said Christina. "We'll either find it or we won't."

"So," Avery explained, "there's a 50 percent chance we'll find it and a 50 percent chance we won't!

"Well," Evan declared, "I think we need a metal detector! We went on a school field trip to a gold mine, and a man showed us how to find things with a metal detector. You sweep it back and forth over the ground, and it beeps when it finds metal."

By this time, the kids had reached the *Mimi*. They scoured the dock and searched under the hammock. No necklace. They turned, **dejected**, and slowly trudged back to the house.

"Arrrrrghhh, maties," cried Evan, "we'll find that buried treasure with this here metal detector! I think I spy some pirate bones!" Skipping ahead, he pretended to sweep the ground with an imaginary wand.

Suddenly, Avery spied something glittering in the mud. Her heart pounded. *It's the necklace!* Her spirits sank when she pick up a jagged piece of shell. Like a thumbtack, it was holding down a ripped piece of lime green paper.

Avery read it to herself.

How weird, thought Avery, tucking the note in her pocket.

BZZZ! BZZZ! "Mimi is texting," said Christina, looking at her cell phone. "She says it's time to get back for our kayak trip."

"I'm so sorry we didn't find it, Christina," said Ella.

"It's a mystery," Christina replied with a forced laugh. "We had a 50-50 chance, but we needed a miracle."

The kids hustled back to Mimi's house. They passed the *Dolphin Catcher,* still tied to the post, still bobbing eerily in the dark water.

Avery thought about the strange note in her pocket and the *Dolphin Catcher. Somehow*

I don't think a dolphin catcher is as harmless as a dream catcher.

Then it occurred to her. Was that the old boat following the dolphins yesterday?

She glared at the scruffy old boat and hurried on.

5

DOLPHIN DREAMS

The tide began to roll in as the golden sun beat down on the sparkling river. Avery shoved her sunglasses up her sweaty nose and pulled down the brim of her pink ball cap.

OK, she thought. *I'm ready for this!*

She dragged her yellow kayak to the water's edge and stepped in like the guide, Eric, had demonstrated. She carefully squeezed down into the kayak seat and jammed her waterproof supply bag under her knees.

"Avery," said Eric. "Take your paddle and push off a little. Steady the boat with your paddle like I showed you."

Christina waved her paddle to Avery from farther out in the water. Christina had kayaked many times. She even had her own pumpkin orange kayak. But this was Avery's first trip. Eric had just given her, Ella, and Evan a paddling lesson on land. Now, they were trying the real thing in the water.

Eric adjusted Evan's foot rudder. "Sweet river shoes, Evan," he said admiringly.

"Thanks!" said Evan, beaming.

Next, Eric tightened Ella's orange life vest. "You're looking good, Ella!" he said.

Eric gently pushed Evan and Ella's royal blue kayaks out into the water. Then, he slid into his own kayak and joined them.

"OK, everyone! Remember what I told you," Eric yelled. "To turn left, push down on the left rudder and paddle on the right. To turn right, push down on the right rudder, and paddle on the left."

"Got it!" said Evan, slowly spinning in a circle.

"We'll just play around here until you feel comfortable," he told the kids. "You all can paddle board so you'll have no trouble with this."

"Do you think we'll see dolphins?" asked Ella.

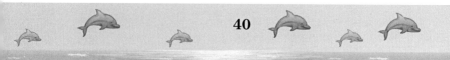

"There's always a good chance of seeing some out here," replied Eric.

"A 50-50 chance?" asked Evan.

"Much better than 50-50!" said Christina. She gave a thumbs-up to her cousin.

"These waters are full of bottlenose dolphins," Eric explained.

"What?" asked Evan. "They have bottles for noses?"

Eric explained that bottlenose dolphins are the type of dolphin found in the warm, coastal waters of North America. "They feed on the fish, squid, and crab that live around here," he said. "They travel in schools of a dozen or so and can swim as fast as 25 miles per hour. So, watch out!"

"They must be smart if they travel in schools," said Evan, giggling at his own joke.

Eric nodded and grinned. "Let's move out now," he said. "The waters are pretty calm, and you're getting the hang of steering. Christina, you stick with Avery. I'll stay with Ella and Evan."

Avery glanced at the compass on her watch and saw that they were heading southeast. She wished she had her iPhone to use the GPS app, but she was afraid to take it out of her waterproof bag. *If I tip over, my phone is doomed,* she thought.

The parade of yellow, blue, and red kayaks floated past tall **spartina** grass swaying in the breeze. The stinky muck gurgled. Hidden clapper rail birds cackled like hyenas.

"It's noisy out here!" Avery shouted to Christina.

Christina pointed her paddle at three wading birds pecking at the ground. "They're looking for lunch!" she yelled.

Minutes later, the group broke toward the open water of the river. Suddenly, Ella screamed, "Dolphins!"

Three muscular gray dolphins glided right past the kayaks. Water glistened on their curved backs. One flipped its tail at Evan, spraying water on him and Ella.

"Ba-Bam!" yelled Evan. His kayak bounced on the waves created by the dolphins.

"Hang on to your paddles, kids!" shouted Eric. "Don't lose them! Don't fight the waves. Just go with them!"

The largest of the three dolphins leaped out of the water between Avery and Christina. "Oh my gosh! It's humongous!" shouted Avery. She was sure the dolphin looked straight at her and smiled. She dipped her paddle deep into the water and paddled as fast as she could. She was joyous! She was paddling alongside wild dolphins!

But the thrill was over as quickly as it had begun. The dolphins leaped again and slipped away, leaving five rocking kayaks in their wake.

"Wow!" shouted Christina, looking stunned. "Did that really just happen to us?"

Avery stared wide-eyed at the disappearing dolphins. But then, something caught her attention in the distance. She gasped. *Is that the old fishing boat? Is it chasing after the dolphins?*

An hour later, the kids were back on shore, chattering all at once to Mimi and Papa about their dolphin experience.

"I know you'll be happy about our Florida plans," said Mimi. "Your mom and dad are heading home with Sadie, and Christina is off to Savannah. We'll leave tomorrow morning for Cocoa Beach, Florida, where there are tons of dolphins! I have research to do for my new book, and you can research your new obsession!"

"Yessss!" cheered Evan. The girls hugged and squealed.

A few hours later, they waved goodbye to their parents and Sadie. Papa helped Christina load her bags into her shiny red Jeep.

"OK," said Christina, "time for hugs from my cousins!"

"I'm still so sorry you lost your necklace," said Avery.

"Me, too," replied Christina. "It's weird—last night, I dreamed I found a dead dolphin on the beach. I cried and cried."

"We'll solve *The Mystery of the Lost Necklace*!" Avery promised.

"Just stay out of trouble!" said Christina. "I know what happens when kids start trying to solve mysteries. Leave the mystery solving to Mimi!"

Christina started her Jeep and slowly drove down the driveway, her hand waving out the window.

Dolphins, dolphin dreams, dolphin boats, and dolphin catchers. Avery had an eerie feeling as she waved goodbye to her cousin. *There really is a mystery here—and it might be bigger than Christina's missing dolphin necklace!*

6

BANANA RIVERS AND CHOCOLATE BEACHES

Within just a few hours, Papa had landed the *Mystery Girl* at Titusville, Florida. The family piled into their rental car for the short drive to Cocoa Beach.

"Over that way," said Papa, pointing to his left, "is Cape Canaveral and the Kennedy Space Center."

"Remember when we watched the movie *Apollo 13* the other night?" asked Mimi. "Cape Canaveral is where that spacecraft was launched!"

Evan's blue eyes grew wide. "Do astronauts live around here?" he asked.

"They do!" replied Mimi. "And they train and work at the Kennedy Space Center."

"Have you ever seen a rocket ship take off, Papa?" asked Ella.

"Only on television," said Papa. "But there's going to be a rocket launch while we're here."

"REALLY?" Avery asked. "Can we see it, Papa? Please?"

"I was hoping you'd want to go with me," said Papa, winking at Mimi.

"Are they going to the moon this time?" asked Ella.

"No, they haven't launched any rockets to the moon for a long time," replied Papa. "The rocket we'll see is carrying cargo and crew supplies to the International Space Station."

"Cool!" said Ella. "I want to take pictures!"

Papa turned the car onto a long bridge arching over shimmering water with tiny whitecap waves.

"We're leaving the mainland of Florida, now," Mimi announced.

Avery rolled down her window. The hot, sticky air whipped her hair around her face. She was daydreaming about going to the moon when, suddenly, she bolted upright. "Look, there are dolphins swimming in that water!" she cried.

Ella and Evan strained to look out Avery's window as a parade of dolphins rolled along the river below them.

"That's the Indian River," said Mimi, looking at Papa's GPS. "Next, we'll cross the Banana River. The ocean and Cocoa Beach are ahead of us. You'll see plenty of dolphins while we're here."

"A banana river!" cried Evan, bumping heads with Ella as he tried to peer out her window from his spot in the middle of the back seat. "I want to see! I want to see! I've never seen a banana river. Between a banana river and a cocoa beach, this is my favorite place ever!!"

"Ah, Evan, I hate to break it to you," said Avery. "But the river is not made out of bananas. That's just its name—the Banana River."

"And," said Mimi, "Cocoa Beach is not made of chocolate. But it's a beautiful beach just the same!"

Evan scrunched up his face and stuck out his chin. "That's just not right," he said. "I wanted to see a cocoa beach!"

Papa tried to cheer up his grandson. "How about we get some bananas and chocolate and take them back to the beach house?" said Papa, pulling up to a grocery store. "Mimi can make banana splits this evening."

"Will you, Mimi?" asked Evan.

"Of course, my sweet boy," said Mimi, patting his arm. "I understand what a disappointment this must be for you."

Avery swung open her car door. An old, beat-up pickup truck was parked in the next space. Fishing gear and nets were scattered across the bed of the rusted, red truck. A huge silver boat hitch stuck out from its rear bumper.

Whew! she thought. *What an ugly truck! That old thing sure smells like ocean and fish!*

Later, when the group emerged from the store loaded down with groceries, the truck was gone. On the ground beside Papa's car, Avery saw a familiar-looking piece of lime green paper.

She picked it up and read to herself:

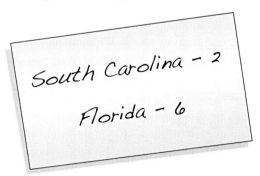

South Carolina - 2

Florida - 6

She reached in her pocket and pulled out the note she had found in Palmetto Bluff. *This is creepy. They're both written on the same lime paper!*

Avery crammed both notes deep down into the pocket of her shorts. She stared at the empty space where the old truck had parked. The foul smell of ocean and fish still lingered in the late afternoon air.

Avery's shoulders shuddered as a chill ran down her spine.

7

SAND OVER MUCK

Mimi opened all the windows of the freshly painted, sunshine-yellow house on Cocoa Beach. Sheer gauze curtains billowed in the ocean breeze. The sounds of squawking sea gulls and waves breaking on the beach filled the house.

"I'm unpacked," Evan announced, stretching a striped t-shirt over his blond head. "I'm ready to explore this place!"

He leaped up on the top bunk bed, dangled his scrawny legs over the edge, and wiggled his toes.

"What are you doing?" asked Ella.

"I'm practicing wiggling my toes in warm sand," Evan replied. "No pluff mud for me today!"

"Thank goodness," said Ella. "I had to throw away my other flip-flops. How do you like these?" she asked, slipping her feet into new turquoise sandals.

"No opinion," said Evan. "I'm a guy. Flip-flops are flip-flops."

Avery hurried through the door, wearing her orange-and-white polka-dot bathing suit and carrying her backpack. "I've got something I need to show you," she said, holding out the two notes.

She explained how she'd found the first note at Palmetto Bluff when they were looking for Christina's necklace. Then, she found the second note next to an old truck that smelled like fish at the grocery store. She read them both aloud to the kids.

"So?" said Evan, shrugging his shoulders.

"I don't mean to be unsupportive here, Avery," said Ella, using her best grownup voice. "But there's a lot of lime green paper in the world! AND there are probably a whole lot of old trucks that smell like fish in Florida!"

"I don't have the slightest idea what that boss note is about," said Evan. He read the second note again. "But this one's a ball score." He scratched his head and put one hand on his chin. "I just can't figure out what kind of game South Carolina and Florida are playing right now. Let's ask Papa."

"No, I don't want to ask Papa right now," said Avery quickly "Let's go explore the beach!"

"Maybe we'll find some dolphins!" said Ella.

Avery carefully tucked the two notes in her backpack and thought, *Why do I want to keep these notes?* But something told her there was a strange connection between the notes and Christina's necklace. *But what?*

8

FISHY, SMELLY OLD TRUCK

"Is it OK if we go out to explore?" Avery asked Mimi, who was busy unpacking groceries.

"Yes, but stay close," said Mimi. "Is everyone wearing sunscreen? And do you have hats?"

"Yes, Mimi," chimed Avery and Ella.

"Don't worry, Captain Mimi," said Evan, saluting her. "We are prepared! And we will rid this area of all suspicious characters. You are safe with us!"

"Just watch for my texts when it's time to come home, Lieutenant!" said Mimi, saluting back.

The kids traipsed out the side porch door and immediately ran into a girl in a yellow bathing suit, pulling an aqua paddle board. She had cocoa-colored skin and long, dark, wavy hair pulled back in a ponytail.

"Hi, I'm Cora Jean Hunter," she said. Her brown eyes sparkled. "Welcome to Cocoa Beach!"

Avery introduced herself, Ella, and Evan. "We just got here!" Avery said. "We came with our grandparents, Mimi and Papa."

"My grandma lives right here," said Cora, pointing to the house next door. "I come down every summer to stay with her. I live in Pittsburgh, Pennsylvania."

"Is it the pits to live in Pittsburgh?" asked Evan, giggling at his joke.

"Don't pay any attention to him, Cora," said Avery. "He likes to joke around."

"That's OK," said Cora. "He's funny! And I love living in Pittsburgh!"

"Isn't it really cold in the winter?" asked Ella.

"It's cold, but it's fun!" replied Cora. "I love to play in the snow and ice skate. It's a whole lot different from here in Florida."

"I bet I would be a good ice skater," said Ella, twirling around.

"Pittsburgh is known as the Steel City because we have so many steel factories," said Cora. "But we also have lots of rivers. Three rivers come together right in the middle of Pittsburgh. I kayak with my family all the time on the rivers."

"Really? We just learned to kayak at our grandparents's house in South Carolina," said Avery. "It was really fun!"

"We want to learn more about dolphins," added Ella. "We saw some when we were kayaking."

"You should have seen them!" yelled Evan. "Those dolphins went flying past us. I was hanging onto my kayak for dear life. I was rocking and swaying. Then I took my paddle and started paddling like mad! I was racing down the river with those dolphins." Evan scampered all around the girls, pretending he was paddling.

The girls giggled. Evan made a big sweeping bow and fell down in the sand, exhausted.

"I'm a dolphin fan, too," said Cora. "This is one of the best places to see dolphins, you know."

"You're a Dolphins fan?!" Evan exclaimed. Clumps of sand flew off his swim trunks as he jumped back up. "I thought you'd be a Pittsburgh Steelers fan. I'm a big Miami Dolphins fan, actually. I bet your friends in Pittsburgh are mad at you!"

"No, no," said Cora. She started laughing. "I mean dolphin dolphins! You know, the mammals, not the Miami Dolphins. I'm no football team traitor!"

"Oh, I get it now," Evan said. "I've never known anyone who was a Steelers fan."

"Well, you do now," said Cora. "And I know a lot about dolphin dolphins!"

"Where can we see some dolphins?" asked Avery.

"I have a secret place," said Cora. "The only other person who knows about it is my grandma. We discovered it last summer. It's

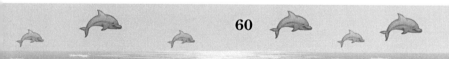

real close to here. I'll ask Grandma if I can take you there. It's a little inlet on the Banana River. The dolphins like to hide and play there!"

Evan froze. Avery's mouth dropped open. Ella's eyes grew wide.

"Do dolphins really PLAY there?" exclaimed Avery.

"Sure," said Cora. "The same dolphins come back all the time. I guess they know they're safe there."

Avery looked quizzical. "What do you mean by safe?" Suddenly, she stopped talking.

An old, rusted pickup truck rumbled slowly down the road behind the beach house. A man wearing a ball cap, fishing vest, and dark sunglasses was driving. Avery caught a whiff of ocean and fish.

She gasped. *It's that fishy, smelly old truck from the grocery store parking lot,* she thought. She could tell the man was watching them from behind his dark sunglasses. *What is he looking for?* Her stomach flipped.

Cora gets mixed up in a
mystery when she meets
Avery, Ella, and Evan.

9

DOLPHIN WISHES

By now, it was late afternoon. Avery, Ella, Evan, and Cora strolled along Cocoa Beach. Cora had given each of them a small bucket for shelling.

"This is the perfect time of day to go shelling," said Cora, gently placing a reddish-brownish scallop shell in her red bucket. "The tide is going out, and there are lots of pretty shells and little clams. Most of the tourists have left the beach for the day so there's not a lot of competition!"

"I like this one," said Ella, holding up a perfect white clam shell.

"It's always good to look through the wrack," said Cora.

"There's a shell rack?" asked Evan. "Like in a shell store?"

"Not like that," Cora said. "The wrack is this line of debris that is left by the tide. See? Pick through this seaweed. You'll see little sticks and shells. Sometimes I find sponges and sea glass. Grandma and I found a beautiful whelk shell last week."

Avery held up a little spiral-shaped shell that was nearly **translucent**. "You can almost see through this one," she said, carefully tucking it in her yellow pail.

"Did you hear about the dead dolphins washing up on the beaches around here?" asked Cora.

"Dead dolphins?" asked Evan, dropping his blue pail and plopping down in the sand.

"Like in Christina's dream!" said Avery, stunned.

"Who's Christina?" asked Cora.

"She's my cousin," said Avery. "She lost her special dolphin necklace a few days ago. She was so upset. She told me she dreamed she found a dead dolphin."

"That's terrible!" said Cora. "These dead dolphins aren't dreams, though. Scientists think a virus is causing the dolphins to die."

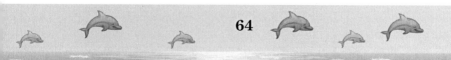

64

"That makes me sad," said Ella.

"I know what I'll do," said Cora. "I have a great idea! Every summer I visit my grandma, we send up a Wish Lantern before I go home."

"What's a Wish Lantern?" asked Ella.

"It's a big, rectangular, paper lantern," said Cora, holding her arms out wide. "It can come in different colors. You unfold it and hold it out. Then, another person uses a lighter to set a small fuel block on fire. Once the lantern expands, you let it go and make a wish as it floats up into the air. The hot air makes it rise."

"Like a hot air balloon?" asked Avery.

"Exactly!" said Cora. "It floats in the air until the flame burns out. Then it falls into the ocean. They're made out of rice paper and bamboo. They eventually disintegrate so they're safe for the environment."

"I want to do that!" said Evan. "Except the fire part. I don't do fire!"

"What is your idea for the dying dolphins?" asked Ella.

"I think maybe this year I'll wish that the dolphins stop dying," said Cora.

"What have you wished for before?" asked Avery.

"Last summer I wished I could swim with the dolphins," replied Cora. "But that hasn't happened yet."

"Oh, that would be my wish, too!" said Avery. She set down her bucket and did a cartwheel in the sand. "I would be so happy!"

"Do you know that dolphins can talk to each other?" asked Cora.

"No way!" cried Evan.

"Yes, way!" said Cora. "They make a clicking sound something like this." Cora pressed her tongue to the back of her lower teeth and made a slight click. "Of course, dolphins can make about 200 clicks a second. I'm lucky if I can do two or three! You just press your teeth with your tongue and click. Try it!"

The kids stood in a circle, trying to click like a dolphin.

"I don't think they would understand me," said Ella.

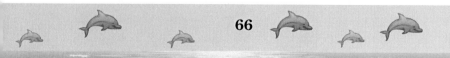

"Actually, I think I have it!" said Evan, imitating a penguin and dancing around.

"My mouth feels like cotton," complained Avery.

"Now, you show me how to do a cartwheel," said Cora to Avery.

"Sure!" said Avery.

She ran a couple steps, gave a little leap, and spun in a perfect cartwheel. With a flourish, she bowed to the group. That's when she saw a handmade sign tacked to a splintered wooden post stuck in the sand.

"Oh, my gosh!" she yelled.

Cora, Ella, and Evan crowded around her and stared, too.

Suddenly, a chilly wind started to blow and clouds blocked the setting sun.

BOOM! Thunder rumbled in the distance. Avery felt like someone was watching them. She scanned the area behind them but saw only an empty beach in the darkening light.

10

WHO'S YOUR MIMI?

"I've never seen this sign in my life!" said an astonished Cora. "Why can't we talk to the dolphins?"

"The real question is: who put it here?" said Avery, still looking over her shoulder.

"This is certainly odd," said Ella, putting her hands on her hips. She took her iPod out of her pocket and took a picture of the sign.

CRANK!

The kids jumped when they heard the start of an engine nearby. Avery spotted the beam of headlights and an old truck rumbling down the beach road behind their houses.

"It's that old fishing truck again," whispered Avery.

"What truck are you talking about?" asked Cora.

"It's a truck that was parked next to us at the grocery store," replied Avery. "I found a note that must've fallen out of it. Now, it seems like the driver is watching us!"

Avery pulled the note out of her pocket and showed it to Cora.

"When did South Carolina play Florida?" Cora asked, puzzled.

"See, Avery?" said Evan. "I told you it was a ball score."

"It's NOT a ball score!" said Avery. "It's part of a mystery!"

"I *looove* mysteries!" Cora said.

"Christina says to stay away from mysteries!" Ella warned.

"But it *IS* a mystery!" said Avery. "First, we saw this old fishing boat chasing dolphins. Then, Christina lost her dolphin necklace. Then, we saw a spooky boat called the *Dolphin Catcher.* I think it was the same boat chasing the dolphins. Now, that old, smelly truck is following us! Plus, I found two notes on the same lime green paper—and there's this sign telling us NOT to do what we were just doing. I'm telling you, it's a mystery!"

"That's confusing," said Evan. His stick-straight hair swung as he shook his head.

"Avery, leave the mysteries to Mimi!" said Ella.

"What do you mean by TWO notes?" said Cora, looking confused.

"Avery found the first note in Palmetto Bluff," said Ella, " when we were at Mimi and Papa's house. Show her, Avery!"

Avery was reaching in her pocket for the other note when Cora shouted, "Palmetto Bluff? Palmetto Bluff, South Carolina? Are you guys from Palmetto Bluff? My OTHER grandma lives there!"

"That's where our Mimi and Papa live," said Avery.

"Wait a minute!" said Cora. "Who's your Mimi?"

"Mimi's name is Carole Marsh," said Ella proudly. "She's the famous author of children's mysteries."

"You are not going to believe this!" said Cora. "I KNOW your Mimi! I met her in Palmetto Bluff at the Palmetto Bluff Inn where my other grandma works. We had lunch together."

"Wow!" Avery and Ella were amazed at the **coincidence**.

BOOM! CRACK!! Lightning zigzagged across the sky.

"We better run!" said Cora. "These summer storms pop up quickly in Florida. We need to get away from this lightning fast. It's dangerous!"

BZZZ! BZZZ! "Yes, we better," shouted Avery, starting to run. "There's Mimi texting me, telling us to get back NOW!"

Raindrops splattered faster and faster as the kids sprinted back to their houses. Their shell buckets clattered as they ran.

Avery waved to Cora as the rain pelted her shoulders and face.

This is fate, she thought. *We are all here together. Cora knows Mimi. Cora knows about dolphins. Now, I'm certain there is a dolphin mystery going on! We just have to connect the clues...*

BOOM!!! CRACK!!!

Avery bolted into the beach house as the rain poured down.

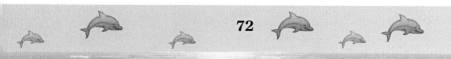

11

COCOA EVERYWHERE

Evan crammed another forkful of scrambled eggs into his mouth. He swallowed a big swig of orange juice.

"You might want to slow down, mister!" said Mimi. "There's plenty more where that came from."

Evan burped and grinned at his grandmother.

KNOCK KNOCK KNOCK!! Avery scurried to the front door.

"We're so happy you're here," she said to Cora. "Mimi can't wait to see you again!"

"Coco Cora!" cried Mimi, holding out her arms. "I can't believe you are right next door to us!"

"Coco Cora?" questioned Ella.

"That's what my Palmetto Bluff grandma calls me," said Cora shyly.

"It's because of her beautiful cocoa-colored skin," said Mimi.

"Coco Cora! Cocoa Beach!" whined Evan. "Chocolate, chocolate, everywhere and not a bite to eat!"

The girls and Mimi laughed.

"How about some of these for dessert?" asked Mimi.

She picked up a plate of warm homemade brownies with chocolate icing and placed it on the table in front of Evan.

"Dessert for breakfast!" shouted Evan. "YESSS!!" He grabbed one with a napkin and pumped his free fist in the air.

"Papa and I have a nice surprise," announced Mimi. "We're taking you on a dolphin cruise later this afternoon. Cora, we would love to have you come along."

Avery and Ella squealed. "That would be so much fun!"

"Yes, please, Mrs. Marsh," said Cora. "Thank you! I just need to ask my grandma."

"Look, Mimi!" said Evan. He tapped on Mimi's laptop and clicked "PLAY" on a YouTube video of dolphins. "These dolphins are talking to each other!"

"We can do it, too!" said Evan excitedly. "Cora showed us!" He tried to make clicking noises, but all he did was spit down his chin. "Why is it not working?" he asked, flopping down in his chair.

"Just keep practicing," said Cora, clicking again. "You'll get it."

"I've heard that dolphins are second only to humans in smarts," said Mimi. "They're very aware of their surroundings, just like we are. And just like humans, they feel hurt and pain mentally, as well as physically."

"Look here," said Evan, pointing to the computer screen. "It says dolphins sleep with one eye open so they won't drown while sleeping."

"That's right," said Cora. "Half of the dolphin's brain goes to sleep while the other half stays awake so it can keep breathing."

"And a dolphin breathes through this blowhole in the top of its head," said Evan, pointing to the screen again.

"That's like our nose!" said Ella.

"But a dolphin only has one hole," said Evan. "We have two! See?" He put an index finger into each nostril.

"You're gross!" said Ella, backing away from her little brother.

"Mimi, can we walk with Cora to a little inlet?" asked Avery. "She says it's not far, and that dolphins come to play there sometimes."

"Who's going for a walk?" asked Papa. He grabbed a brownie as he joined everyone in the kitchen. "I'd like to explore this area myself."

"Perfect, Papa! You go with the kids, and I'll go over right now and ask Cora's 'Florida grandma' if she can go on the cruise with us," said Mimi. She glanced in a mirror and fluffed her short blond hair. "I can't wait to meet her!"

The kids scurried out the door with Papa strolling behind. Avery was excited, but she wasn't excited to think the man in the old truck might be hanging around. *Is he spying on us?*

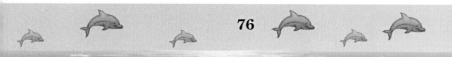

12

DOLPHIN COVE

The kids picked their way along the sandy path that led to Cora's secret inlet. Palm trees, sage palmetto, and wetland marsh grasses grew wild and thick. A mangrove cuckoo sang from his hidden perch in the swamp. A tall, graceful crane observed them quietly. Avery watched a hawk swoop to land on a low tree branch.

"I feel like I'm in the jungle," said Ella.

"Cora, have you ever seen a rocket launch?" Evan asked.

"I've never watched one," replied Cora, "but I've heard them. They're pretty loud. I think I heard on the news there's a launch tomorrow morning."

"I'd really like to go to space someday," said Ella.

All the kids agreed.

"Ssshhh!!" said Cora, stopping and holding her finger to her lips. "Do you hear it?"

"Space?" said Evan. "I've never heard it, but I've seen plenty of pictures on the Internet."

"I don't mean space!" said Cora. "The dolphins! Can you hear the dolphins?"

Somewhere ahead of them, they could hear faint clicking and splashing.

"Let's be quiet," whispered Cora. "They're not used to anyone except me and Grandma. We'll take it slow."

The kids tiptoed through the underbrush. The sounds of dolphins at play became a little louder.

Suddenly, they reached a clearing in the dense **foliage** where the inlet's blue water sparkled ahead of them.

Cora placed her finger to her lips again and slowly stepped into the clearing. Avery, Ella, and Evan followed her on tiptoes.

The kids gasped. Before them, a pod of about a dozen dolphins clicked and splashed in the inlet. They slid elegantly in and out of the water. They leaped gracefully in the air. A few even somersaulted backwards, landing with a huge SPLASH in the rippling water.

"It's like kids playing in a swimming pool," whispered Avery. "They look like they're having a blast!"

Cora motioned the kids to sit on a moss-covered rock at the edge of the inlet. She stood quietly until the dolphins saw her. One by one, they glided toward her and back into the center of the inlet, flipping and splashing. One dolphin raised up out of the water, its tail moving furiously to keep itself upright. The dolphin clicked **incessantly** as if to say hello.

Cora clicked back a couple of times and bent down closer to the water. She waved at them. The dolphins all began to click at once.

"Come over here," she said to the kids. "They understand you're with me. They aren't scared."

The kids moved slowly toward Cora, still stunned at the dolphin display they had just witnessed. "I can't believe how big they are," said Ella, wide-eyed.

Within a few minutes, kids and dolphins were playing side by side. The dolphins somersaulted and clicked in the water. The kids leaped and tumbled on the ground near the shore of the inlet. They were friends!

"Look at me!" cried Evan, attempting a flip, but ending up rolling in the grass.

Avery, the cheerleader, showed him how a flip was done. "We can call it the dolphin flip," she said, springing back on her feet.

"I got it!" said Cora suddenly. "It seems so simple now. I've never known what to call this place, but how about Dolphin Cove?"

"Perfect," said Ella, spinning around. "Dolphin Cove!"

"Have you ever seen anyone else here?" Avery asked Cora.

"Never," said Cora.

"I have this funny feeling we should keep it a secret," said Avery, looking around.

"You're probably right," said Cora. "I've never told anyone except you guys."

"Are the same dolphins always here?" asked Ella, huffing as she ran up to Cora. Her hair stuck to her sweaty forehead.

"This summer, I think it's been mostly the same ones," replied Cora. "Dolphins pretty much live and travel in their own little group."

"They have such big heads," said Ella.

"That's called their melon," said Cora.

"Hey!" cried Evan. "That's what Papa says to me about my head—that I have a big melon!" He thumped his finger against the side of his head.

"What are the fins called?" asked Avery.

"The fin in the center of its back is called the dorsal fin," replied Cora. "It helps to balance the dolphin in the water. The fins on each side of its body are called pectoral fins. They help the dolphin stop and steer. The tail fin is also called the fluke. Dolphins lift themselves out of the water by using their tail flukes."

"Look at those two silly ones!" said Evan. He pointed at two dolphins balancing on their tails up out of the water and clicking repeatedly at each other.

"I always see those two," said Cora.

"How do you tell them from the others?" asked Ella.

"For one thing, they are ALWAYS side by side," said Cora. "The one on the left is a little larger and has a chunk taken out of his fin. The other smaller one is much darker, almost black."

"I see what you mean," said Avery, studying the dolphins.

"Some of the others, I'm not so sure about," said Cora. "I think their faces look a little different or they sound different. But I know those two. They're always jabbering!"

"They look like they're playing a game," said Evan, "like Marco Polo."

"What's that?" asked Cora.

"You know, that swimming game," said Avery. "The player who is 'It' closes his eyes and shouts 'Marco.' The other players have to answer by shouting 'Polo.' The 'It' player has to find someone to tag using only his hearing!"

Cora snapped her fingers. "I have a fantastic idea!" she exclaimed. "I've always wanted to name those two dolphins. Let's name the bigger one Marco, and the smaller one Polo."

"I like it!" said Avery.

BZZZ! "It's a text from Mimi," said Avery. "It's time to get back so we can go on the dolphin cruise!"

"Goodbye, Marco!" yelled Evan.

"Goodbye, Polo!" yelled Ella.

The kids waved to the dolphins and scurried up the path to meet Papa. Ahead, through the foliage, they spotted a man wearing a ball cap and a fishing vest. The door of his old, rusty pickup truck creaked as he stepped into it.

"Get down!" hissed Avery. "That's the old truck that's been following us!"

The kids hid in the swaying beach grass and watched the truck back out of the brush and disappear down the beach road.

The kids looked at each other.

"This is serious," whispered Evan.

Avery nodded. *Evan is right. The secret of Dolphin Cove is out!*

Bottlenose dolphins produce
whistles and other sounds like
clicks, squeaks, and grunts!

13

SPINNERS AND LEAPERS

"There are as many as 800 dolphins that cruise this Indian River Lagoon system on Florida's Space Coast," stated the Dolphin Cruise captain into his microphone. "These bottlenose dolphins are the most common and well-known type of dolphins."

The captain looked straight at Evan. "Young man, did you know the killer whale, also known as orca, is actually a type of dolphin?"

Evan gulped. "No, sir, I did not!"

"Dolphins have about 100 teeth," said the captain, "and they are carnivores. Do you know what that means, young man?"

"No, sir," replied Evan, backing away from the captain toward Mimi.

"That means they eat meat!" said the captain loudly.

"Mimi," said Evan, "I think I'm on dolphin overload." He plunked down on Mimi's lap. "And why does he keep asking *ME* those questions?"

Mimi laughed and tousled his blond hair. "You just got lucky, I guess!"

Avery, Cora, and Ella leaned on the rail of the cruiser. In the distance, they spied dolphins playing, just like the ones in Dolphin Cove.

"Look!" shouted Ella, pointing toward the dolphins. "What is that one doing?"

People stretched their necks to see a dolphin leaping into the air and twirling around.

"That's known as a spinner dolphin," announced the captain. "They are a special kind of dolphin that have a whirling and twirling motion. Most other dolphins can somersault or flip head over tail. A spinner dolphin is the only one that can spin with its nose pointed to the sky and its tail to the water."

"I wonder if any of these dolphins have ever been to Dolphin Cove," whispered Avery. Cora and Ella grinned at the thought.

Just then, an enormous charcoal-colored dolphin leaped out of the water right next to the railing where the girls stood. Water spewed from its blowhole. A wave of warm saltwater hit the cruiser's deck.

"That is your bottlenose dolphin—up close and personal!" announced the captain. "The average Atlantic bottlenose dolphin is about eight-and-a-half feet long and weighs between 400 and 500 pounds. It lives in saltwater rivers, bays, **estuaries**, marshes, and in the open ocean. It can jump up to twenty feet above water, and can hold its breath for about five to seven minutes. Say 'hello,' folks!"

Papa leaned over the rail and tipped his big black cowboy hat as the dolphin leaped away. Evan pumped his fist in the air. "Hello, dolphin!" he cried. The girls laughed, and Mimi blew a kiss.

An hour later, the dolphin cruiser floated into its home pier.

"I feel like I'm still on the boat!" said Avery, swaying as she walked. She glanced down to the end of the dock and spotted another boat tied there.

Horrified, she whispered to Ella and Cora. "It's the *Dolphin Catcher*! It was in Palmetto Bluff, and now it's HERE!"

Evan crept up behind her and handed her a piece of paper. "Hey, I found this," he said. It was lime green.

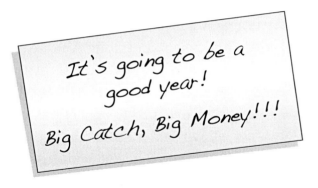

It's going to be a good year!

Big Catch, Big Money!!!

Avery looked at the kids and said, "We have to get back to Dolphin Cove! I have the feeling that something is very, very wrong!"

14

BONES AND MANGROVES

The kids raced down the sandy path to Dolphin Cove. They spotted Marco and Polo right away, but some of the dolphins from the morning were missing.

"They might be looking for food," said Cora. "Grandma says dolphins use something called echolocation to navigate and hunt. They make sounds underwater and listen for the echoes of those sounds. The echoes help them find the exact location of objects and food."

"What do they eat?" asked Evan.

"They eat a lot of squid," said Cora, "and other fish, like mackerel and mullet."

"I've never had a mullet," said Evan, patting down his blond hair. "Mom wouldn't let me when I asked her."

Cora laughed at Evan, while Avery and Ella just shook their heads.

"Grandma told me that bigger dolphins can eat as much as 50 pounds of fish a day!" said Cora.

"Fifty pounds is a lot of fish," said Ella.

"I still don't feel good about this," said Avery. "Just my intuition."

"What's your too-ish-in?" asked Evan, cocking his head to one side.

"IN-tuition," said Avery. "It's an instinct. It's like a sixth sense. It's something I feel in my bones!"

"I can feel my bones!" said Evan. He spread his fingers over his ribs. "Actually, I can feel a lot of bones. See?"

Evan patted his knobby knees. He was reaching down to feel his ankle when Avery interrupted his fun.

"That's not quite what I mean, Evan," she said impatiently, glancing around the cove.

"My too-ish-in in my arm says they're out playing in the river," said Evan, rubbing his elbow.

"Look at these **shenanigans!**" said Cora. "I think Marco and Polo are trying to tell us something."

The dolphins lifted themselves high up out of the water and clicked with ear-splitting intensity. Then, they dove into the water, leaped back out, flipped their tails, and swam furiously to where the cove merged into the river. After that, they glided back to the kids— and started the process all over again.

"What do you think they're saying?" asked Avery.

"I'll take a video of them," said Ella.

She aimed her iPod at the dolphins and walked backward a few steps. Suddenly, she stumbled and fell into the wet grass.

"Are you OK?" asked Avery, running to her sister.

"I knocked over a sign," said Ella.

"A sign!" said Avery and Cora together.

"What's so bad about a little sign?" asked Evan.

"That sign means someone's been here!" said Avery.

Ella stood up and brushed herself off. A piece of cardboard stapled to a wood stake lay flat on the ground.

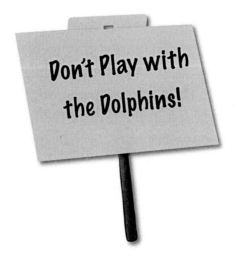

Don't Play with the Dolphins!

"Who would put a sign here?" said Cora, panicking. "No one even knows about Dolphin Cove, except us!"

"This is creepy," said Ella. "I don't like it."

She opened her photo folder on her iPod. "First, a sign that said 'Don't Talk to the Dolphins.' Now, another one!"

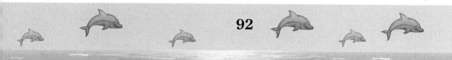

SNAP! She took a photo of the second sign. Marco and Polo continued to chatter insistently in the background.

Ella turned to Avery. "You're right, Avery," she said quietly. "This *is* a mystery. And I think someone is watching us." She took Avery's hand.

The sun was sinking in the sky, and it was growing dark. The gray dolphins began to disappear into the shadiness of the cove. The dark shadows of mangrove trees with their tangled roots looked like spooky characters in a horror movie.

Are dolphins missing? thought Avery. *Where are these signs coming from? Is the man in the old truck really watching us?*

Avery surveyed Dolphin Cove and shuddered. "Let's get out of here!" she said.

15

DREAMS OR NIGHTMARES

"Here's a picture of the rocket that's taking off in the morning," said Ella, looking at a news website on Mimi's laptop. "It says it's taking supplies to the International Space Station."

The kids sat at the beach house kitchen table, finishing their dessert of apple cobbler and vanilla ice cream.

"Did you find a design for a rocket ship we can use with the 3D printer yet?" asked Evan.

"No, not yet," replied Ella. "Maybe we can create a design of our own and print it."

Mimi had surprised them with a new 3D printer that could create three-dimensional

objects. Ella had found a dolphin design on the Internet and had downloaded it to the printer. Now, Evan intently watched as the printer layered strands of blue plastic into a three-dimensional dolphin.

"That is so cool!" Evan exclaimed. "I can't wait to take my 3D dolphin home to show all my friends!"

"I have to say I'm impressed with you kids and your newfangled stuff," Papa said. "As my daddy used to say, 'What'll they think of next?' Now, where's Mimi?"

"She's sitting on the beach," said Avery. "Red-striped chair!"

Papa waved and strolled out the door.

"We need to look at these clues," said Avery. She placed the three green notes on the table.

"Here," said Ella. "I printed out photos of the signs." She laid the photos on the table beside the notes.

"Notes and signs," said Avery. "We have a man in an old pickup truck who seems to be following us. Then, there's that dreadful *Dolphin Catcher* we saw in Palmetto Bluff and here."

"The *ghooooost* boat!" said Evan.

"I need to secretly take a picture of the truck and the boat," said Ella.

"Then, there's missing dolphins and Christina's missing necklace!" said Avery.

The kids stared intently at the clues and then at Avery.

"Now what?" asked Cora.

"Avery, I think there's some kind of mystery here," said Ella. "Especially if dolphins are missing. And it's weird and scary for us to find the green notes and the signs. But what does Christina's necklace have to do with this? She lost it in Palmetto Bluff."

Avery shrugged. "I've just got a hunch it's all tied together," she said. "And something is terribly wrong!"

Just then, Mimi burst into the room. Avery quickly shoved the photos and notes into her backpack.

"Surprise!!" said Mimi. "After the rocket launch in the morning, Papa is going to fly us all down to Marathon, Florida. I've arranged for us to swim with the dolphins. Cora's going, too!"

The kids whooped and hollered.

"My wishing lantern wish is coming true!" cried Cora, jumping up and down.

Avery hugged Mimi around the waist. *Wouldn't it be fun to swim with Marco and Polo,* she thought. But then a wave of fear surged through her body. *Are dreams coming true, or is this a nightmare?*

16

ROCKETS AND PREDATORS

As the ground shuddered beneath their feet, the kids clapped their hands over their ears to shut out the deafening roar. White steamy smoke billowed around the base of the rocket. Pieces of metal scaffolding tumbled from the rocket's gleaming white cylinder as the craft lifted up into the bright morning sky.

"Wow!" yelled Evan.

"Double wow!" yelled Mimi.

Everyone kept their eyes glued to the hot-white glow and fiery trail of the spacecraft until it disappeared into the clouds.

"What an experience!" said Papa. "That was worth getting up early for!"

"Why is there so much smoke, Papa?" asked Ella.

"The burning rocket fuels produce hot gases that come out of the bottom of the rocket," Papa explained. "This provides the force that lifts the rocket off the ground."

"Was anyone driving that thing?" asked Evan.

"No," said Papa. "It's an unmanned resupply ship. It's programmed to orbit the Earth four times and then dock to the International Space Station."

"What's an orbit?" asked Evan.

"In this case, an orbit is the curved path that the spacecraft takes around the Earth," replied Papa. "So, it will go around the Earth four times before it docks with the Space Station."

"Just think," said Mimi with a laugh. "That spacecraft will probably get to its destination before the *Mystery Girl* can get us to Marathon!"

A few hours later, Papa's red and white plane touched down smoothly on the runway in Marathon, Florida.

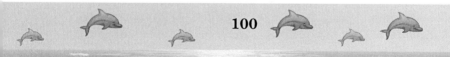

"Nice landing, Papa!" said Evan, patting his grandfather on the shoulder.

"Thanks, buddy," said Papa, tipping his cowboy hat. "This is a pretty narrow chain of islands. They run about 127 miles from the northern tip all the way down to Key West. Marathon is about the halfway point."

"All I can see is water and sand," said Avery, her nose pressed to the window.

"That's about all there is," said Mimi. "The islands are made of sand and ancient coral reefs and surrounded by beautiful aquamarine water. There are lots of unusual plants and animals, and they are surrounded by dolphins!"

Before long, Mimi, Papa, and the kids arrived at the Dolphin Research Center.

"I've always wanted to come here," said Cora. "They study dolphins, but they have a natural environment for them. It's not like typical Florida dolphin attractions."

A slender, dark-haired young woman with a big smile came around the corner. "Welcome to the Dolphin Research Center," said Brianna, their guide. "I heard that you've been learning a lot about dolphins."

"We like to call this our 'Summer of the Dolphin,'" Evan quipped.

"Well, we're going to make this a day to remember!" said Brianna. "I hope you brought your swimsuits because you're booked for a private swim lesson. We're going to have fun!"

First, Brianna took them on a tour of the Center. Their first stop was the outdoor area, where swaying palm trees and thatch-roofed huts surrounded several enormous pool enclosures. Ocean water flowed directly into the pools where dolphins swam, leaped, and splashed.

"We have about 22 dolphins at the Center right now," explained Brianna. "They live in groups comparable to dolphins in the wild. We get to watch their natural behavior and get to know their 'dolphinalities'!"

"Dolphinalities!" exclaimed Cora. "I like that!"

"Now, that can't be a dolphin," said Evan. He stared at a massive, round creature floating in the pool. "He looks like a blob with a head and fins on it!"

"That's not a dolphin," said Brianna. "It's a manatee. As you can see, they are very round and heavy. Some people call them sea cows. They are also very gentle. Manatees are herbivores, which means they eat only plants."

"Isn't the manatee Florida's state marine mammal?" Cora asked.

"Yes, it is!" said Brianna. "The manatee is also one of the most endangered marine mammals in the United States. Part of our purpose here at the Center is to rescue and rehabilitate manatees, dolphins, sea lions, and whales that have been found in distress in the waters around the Keys."

Brianna led the group to an observation deck overlooking the pool area.

"I can't wait to do that," said Cora, watching other visitors play with the dolphins. Avery smiled and nodded. "Me too," she whispered.

"Dolphins are not fish," Brianna explained. "They're mammals, just like you and me. They breathe in air, give birth to live young, and nurse their babies with milk. Did you know they have hair on the top of their

snout, or rostrum, when they're first born? It falls out within two weeks, and they never grow any hair again!"

"Hair? I didn't know that," said Cora.

"What do dolphins drink?" asked Ella. "Seawater?"

"That would be too salty!" said Evan.

"That's a great question," Brianna said. "Dolphins don't drink water. They get all the water they need from the fish they eat."

"Can they see underwater?" asked Avery.

"Bottlenose dolphins have excellent vision above and below water," said Brianna. "They can also see very well at night, just like cats and dogs. Scientists don't think dolphins can see colors, though—just shades of gray."

"That would be like watching black and white television," said Mimi.

"Black and white TV!" said Evan. "How boring!"

"For a long time, dolphins have been a favorite sea creature to humans," Brianna continued. Just then, a dolphin slid by, spewing a blast of air and water out of its

blowhole. "They represent compassion, caring, community, and generous spirit. They always seem to be reaching out to connect with humans. For the most part, people have grown to respect dolphins as powerful, yet graceful, friends who live in the sea."

"Do you know what it means when you dream about a dolphin?" Avery asked Brianna.

"Well, people who analyze dreams say that if you dream you are riding a dolphin, it means you are feeling very optimistic," replied Brianna.

Avery thought about Christina's dream.

"What does it mean if you dream a dolphin is dead or dying?" asked Avery.

"That can indicate a feeling of despair," said Brianna.

"Poor Christina," whispered Ella.

"I just thought of something," said Avery. "Who are the dolphin's predators?"

"What's a pred-a-what?" asked Evan.

"A predator is an animal that naturally preys on other animals," said Brianna. "Predators attack the other animal, usually to feed on it. In the ocean, the only real predators

that dolphins have to worry about are big sharks. Large sharks will prey on weak, slow, sick, and aged dolphins. They pretty much leave the healthy, bigger dolphins alone."

"Then dolphins don't really have many predators," said Cora.

"Unfortunately, a dolphin's main predator is an animal that doesn't live in the ocean," said Brianna.

The kids looked puzzled. "What is it?" Ella asked, concerned.

"Sadly, the dolphin's main predator is humans," said Brianna. "People catch dolphins and sell them to dolphin attractions. Sometimes, the dolphins are so traumatized, they die before they reach the destination."

Avery, Ella, Evan, and Cora stared at Brianna in stunned silence. Avery shuddered—again.

17

DOLPHIN ENCOUNTER

Mimi and four very excited kids waited impatiently in their bathing suits near the dolphin pool. Papa volunteered to take pictures and video with his iPad. He found a spot on a nearby bench and got ready to record the experience.

"This may be the most exciting day of my life!" said Cora, giggling and clapping.

"First," said Brianna, "we're going to get in the water and get used to the dolphins and let them get used to us."

Mimi and the kids stepped gingerly into the shallow pool. Within a few seconds, friendly, curious dolphins surrounded them. Avery's heart raced and her hands shook. The dolphins splashed Mimi and the kids, and they cautiously splashed them back.

"Can we touch them?" asked Cora.

"Sure!" Brianna replied.

Ella slowly reached her hand to touch a small, light gray dolphin. "They're so soft and slick," she said. "Try it, Avery!"

Avery took a deep breath and slid her hand along the dolphin's back. She giggled with excitement. "I love them!" she cried. "They're so sweet!"

"Take their fins to clap with them," said Brianna. "Come here, Delta," she said to another smaller dolphin. "Show Evan how to clap."

The dolphin stood up on its tail facing Brianna. Brianna grabbed one fin in each of her hands and clapped them together. "You try now, Evan," she said.

Soon, Evan was clapping and giggling with Delta. "Look!" he cried, "We're playing patty-cake!"

Brianna showed Ella how to place her hand under the dolphin's snout and let it kiss her cheek. Ella beamed and waved her arm to get Papa's attention. "See me, Papa! Take a picture!"

After about ten minutes, Brianna asked, "So, who's ready to swim with a dolphin?"

"I'm ready, I'm ready!" exclaimed Cora.

"Stand behind and to the right side of Gypsi here," said Brianna to Cora. "Extend your left arm with your palm out. Now, grab hold of her dorsal fin. That's the fin on the top. Get ready to ride!"

At Brianna's hand signal, the dolphin shot across the swimming area with Cora in tow. Mimi clapped her hands and giggled at Cora's exhilarated smile as Gypsi **escorted** her on several laps around the pool. Finally, Cora and Gypsi glided up to Brianna.

Cora jumped up and down and kissed Gypsi over and over.

"My wish came true!" she shouted.

Ella went next, and then Evan, who got so excited he let go of Gypsi's fin and had to start again.

"I did that on purpose," said Evan when his turn was done. "I just wanted to get some extra swim time." He giggled.

"Your turn, Mimi," said Avery. She watched in admiration as her sassy Mimi swam gracefully around the enclosure with a dolphin named Louie.

"Did you get plenty of pictures, Papa?" asked Mimi when her ride was finished. "I need them for my Facebook page!"

Papa gave a thumbs up sign.

"It's your turn, Avery," said Cora. "You'll love it!"

Avery stepped forward to swim with a dolphin named Calusa. She took Calusa's dorsal fin in her hand. It was soft and slick. At Brianna's signal, Calusa accelerated and carried Avery across the pool. Avery laughed with delight as water sprayed her face.

This is the most exciting thing I've ever done! she thought. For a few minutes, Avery felt like a wild animal herself. She and Calusa were one. She had an urge to head straight for the ocean on the back of Calusa and ride the high seas.

But soon, the ride was over, and images of Dolphin Cove drifted back into her mind.

She heard the rumble of the red pickup truck in her head. *Dolphins are missing. Humans are a dolphin's most dangerous predator. Who is the man in the truck? Does the Dolphin Catcher belong to him, too? We have to get back to Dolphin Cove!*

Even with the bright, tropical sun beating down on Avery, she shivered, and the hair stood up on her arms.

18

MISSING MARCO

Avery charged ahead as she, Cora, Ella, and Evan scrambled down the overgrown path leading to Dolphin Cove.

"Hurry!" called Avery, stumbling over a mangrove root. "I know something is wrong. I can feel it in my bones!"

When they burst into the clearing, they were shocked. Only three dolphins swam slowly around the cove.

"Where are they?" asked Evan fearfully.

"Where are Marco and Polo?" cried Ella.

"There's Polo," cried Cora, "but I don't see Marco anywhere!"

Polo saw the kids and swam swiftly toward them. He lifted his head out of the water and started clicking furiously. His

muscular tail beating rapidly through the water, Polo swam to where the cove opened out into the deep blue ocean. Then he raced back to the kids and clicked incessantly once again. Back and forth, back and forth he went.

"Polo is going crazy!" cried Evan. "He's trying to tell us something!"

"He's worried that Marco is gone," said Avery. "We have to do something!"

That's when she noticed a sign tacked to a small palm tree. She dashed over to it.

"Look at this," she yelled. "Someone has taken Marco and the other dolphins!" said Avery. "That someone is a natural predator of dolphins."

The kids stared at each other, frightened.

Avery turned around to peer at the nearly empty cove and watched Polo race around, clicking and splashing. Her stomach flipped.

"That someone is a man!" she declared.

19

RUN FOR YOUR LIFE

Smoky gray clouds rolled in, darkening the late afternoon sky. Avery led the way as the kids bolted from Dolphin Cove and the discovery they had made.

"I'm sure glad Papa's plane landed before this storm started moving in," said Cora, zipping up her blue jacket.

"Where are we going, Avery?" asked Ella. Her hair kept blowing in her eyes as she tried to keep up.

Avery stopped and whirled to look at the others. "Do you remember what our guide said at the Research Center? Humans are the main natural predator of dolphins. That means a human—some mean, **despicable** person—is taking the dolphins away from Dolphin Cove."

"But who?" asked Evan.

"I don't know," said Avery, "but we have to find out."

"We have to save the dolphins," agreed Cora. "We have to find Marco!"

"What are we going to do?" asked Ella.

"First," said Avery, "we're going back to the pier where the *Dolphin Catcher* was docked. I've always had a bad feeling about that boat. Let's go!"

"But Avery," said Ella, tugging on Avery's lavender rain jacket as they ran, "what are we going to do when we get there? Knock on the door?"

"I don't know," replied Avery, jumping over a piece of driftwood. "I just know Marco is gone. Someone probably took him and the other dolphins away from Dolphin Cove. That same person might be trying to scare us away, too!"

"Maybe...that man...in the stinky old truck...is catching the dolphins!" said Evan, his voice breathless as his skinny legs pumped across the ground.

"It sure is weird how he keeps creeping up on us," agreed Cora.

"We'll figure this out," yelled Avery over her shoulder at the kids. "Christina dreamed she found a dolphin dying on the beach. I don't want that dolphin to be Marco!"

Just then, Avery caught sight of the pier. She sprinted toward it.

"Act cool," said Avery, slowing to a stop. She bent over to catch her breath. Then, she searched for her sunglasses in her backpack and slipped them over her eyes. "We're incognito," she whispered.

"We're not in Cog Nito," Evan whispered back. "We're in Florida!"

"*Incognito* means we're in disguise," said Ella. "We don't want anyone to know who we are. It's like we're spies." She pulled out her own sunglasses and placed them on her nose.

"Oh!" Evan whispered loudly. "But I don't have any sunglasses."

"Here," said Avery, yanking her pink ball cap out of her backpack.

"I'm not wearing a pink hat!" said Evan, folding his scrawny arms over his chest.

"I'll take that," said Cora, snatching the pink cap from Avery.

"How's this, then?" said Avery to Evan. She tossed him her well-worn, beloved Atlanta Braves ball cap.

"Much better," said Evan.

"Don't lose it!" Avery warned.

The group strolled along the pier, chitchatting. Evan enjoyed a sucker he'd found in his pocket. Ella began snapping pictures like a tourist. Avery casually slung her backpack over her shoulder while she **scrutinized** the pier from behind her dark shades.

"I don't see the *Dolphin Catcher* anywhere," Avery whispered.

A man, wearing sunglasses and a beat-up ball cap, suddenly appeared from between two boats. He walked quickly and forcefully toward them. When he got closer, he said, "You kids got no business on this pier without your parents."

Avery looked hard at him. *Is this the man from the truck?* She couldn't tell.

"Yes, sir," said Ella politely.

"Then skedaddle!" said the man, passing them by and hurrying on.

"There's the *Dolphin Catcher*," Cora whispered, pointing at the end of the pier. The rickety boat gently bobbed up and down in the water.

"I don't care what he says," said Ella, trotting down the pier to get closer to the boat. "Let's take a picture!"

The kids dashed after her. Ella quickly lined them up for a selfie in front of the *Dolphin Catcher.*

"Hey!" the man hollered, heading back in their direction. "I told you kids to get out of here!"

"We're leaving, sir," said Ella. "We just wanted some pictures. We're just visiting."

"I don't care where you're from!" he barked. "Get off the dock!"

Just then, the *Dolphin Catcher*'s engine cranked. The kids darted past the man to get off the pier.

"Avery!" said Ella, as they left the pier and started down the road. "Look what I found on the pier!" The kids gathered around to study the coffee-stained piece of paper.

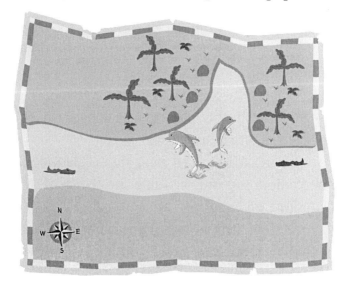

"Is that a treasure map?" Evan asked.

"No! That's a map of Dolphin Cove!" gasped Cora.

Avery stuffed it in her pocket as raindrops started to fall.

Avery and Ella go incognito to solve the mystery!

20

THE CHASE

The kids huddled in Cora's grandmother's boathouse as raindrops clattered on the metal roof.

"Here's the plan," said Avery. "Cora and I will put in our kayaks here, and paddle around to Dolphin Cove. We'll hide in the marsh and watch to see if we can tell what's happening to the dolphins. Ella, you and Evan stay here. I will text you if we have any trouble."

"No!" said Ella, putting her hands on her hips. "I'm going, too. If you don't let me go, I'll tell Mimi."

Avery sighed. She could tell her stubborn little sister meant what she said. "OK, Ella," Avery said, "but stay close to me. Evan, you go back to the house and hang out with Mimi."

"I can do that!" said Evan.

"Here," said Cora, handing Ella an extra life vest. "Grandma has plenty of these because she has lots of visitors." Then she handed a headlamp to Avery to fasten around her forehead. Ella couldn't help but giggle at the sight. "You look like a real nerd!"

Avery was all business. "Better to look like a nerd and solve the mystery than look cool and be clueless," she said.

"I've got a couple of little flashlights," said Cora, handing one to Ella. "Don't waste the battery in your iPod."

The girls gingerly stepped into their kayaks and used their paddles to push away from the shoreline.

"Evan, we'll text you if there's any trouble," said Avery, waving goodbye to her little brother. "Cora, Ella and I will follow you."

"It's not far," said Cora. "We'll paddle through this little canal to get to the river. Then, on the river, all we have to do is stay close to the water's edge."

The three girls steered their kayaks toward Dolphin Cove. The sky was overcast. Fine, light raindrops cast thousands of ripples on the water. The kids heard no sounds except the raindrops, the swish of water lapping against the shore, and the paddles pushing through the marsh.

"Dolphin Cove is right over here," called Cora, pointing.

Wow, thought Avery. *We're coming into Dolphin Cove like the dolphins do.*

CLICK! CLICK! It was Polo! He popped up out of the water just ahead of them.

"Hush, Polo," said Cora. She clicked a couple of times.

They quickly followed Polo in their kayaks until Cora held up one hand, motioning the girls to stop.

Avery immediately understood why.

In the semi-darkness, the *Dolphin Catcher* emerged from Dolphin Cove and slid slowly away from them.

"We can't lose that boat!" yelled Avery.

128

21

POLO LEADS THE WAY

Evan sprinted as fast as his scrawny legs would carry him. Rain pelted his body. His t-shirt was soaked by the time he reached Dolphin Cove. He slid into the shadows of a mangrove tree and perched on its bony roots to watch. In the darkness, he could barely see an old fishing boat. He heard splashing and furious dolphin clicking—and the deep voices of men.

I bet that's the haunted ghost boat. Those varmint pirates!

The fishing boat's motor cranked, shattering the stillness of the cove. Evan watched the boat back slowly out of the cove and putt down the river.

Where's Avery? he thought. Just then, he spied the **silhouettes** of three kayakers paddling past the mouth of Dolphin Cove.

On no! Evan was horrified. *They're chasing after the boat.* "What am I going to dooooo?" he bellowed into the stillness of the empty cove. Evan raced off again, running as if someone was chasing him, too.

The girls paddled quickly behind the *Dolphin Catcher*, doing their best to keep it in sight. Polo glided effortlessly beside them. The huge dolphin was not playing now. He stayed alongside Avery's kayak, dipping into the water every so often, and coming back up for air.

He looks so sad, Avery thought. *Don't be sad, Polo. We'll find Marco.*

The rain splattered down harder now. The waves rose higher and rougher. Deepening fog and sheets of rain made it harder to keep the *Dolphin Catcher* in sight.

The girls steadily drew closer to the boat. Then, Avery realized the boat was slowing down. It stopped alongside a broken-

down pier. Avery watched a dark figure clamber out of the boat and anchor it to an old post. The faint sound of country music drifted in the air. She noticed a rundown, square-shaped boat tied up to the pier as well. It looked like a houseboat, but didn't have a roof on it.

Then she heard it, even in the pouring rain—the distinct sound of clicking and squeaking.

Dolphins!

Now I know what's happening, thought Avery. She edged her kayak past Cora. Faster and faster she raced against the bouncing currents toward the old pier. Her kayak rocked as her paddles tore into the surface of the water.

The rain pelted her face but she could still see the gray blur of Polo churning up the water ahead. Cora and Ella furiously paddled behind her. Her heart was thumping!

 **132**

22

NETS AND BUCKETS

The bow of the *Dolphin Catcher* began to slide away from the pier.

"Hey, get out here and help me," yelled the man, tying up the boat. "You afraid of getting wet or something?"

Another man appeared on the deck of the ghostly boat. He reached down and threw a coil of heavy rope at the man on the pier.

"Quit your complaining!" he grumbled. "I'm the brains of this operation. You should be able to tie up a little boat by yourself."

A petite woman in yellow overalls and black rubber fishing boots appeared from the other side of the square-shaped boat. She stood on the pier and started throwing fish out of a bucket and into the top of the roofless houseboat.

"I hope you didn't bring too many back!" she grumbled to the two men. "We can't get many more in this holding area. We need to deliver what we have and get our money."

"We got two more," said the first man. "Woulda' had three, but one got away!"

"BE QUIET!!!" the woman screeched as she tossed more fish into the center of the roofless houseboat. "I can't take any more of these clicking noises. I hate these fish!"

"I keep telling you, Myrtle," yelled the second man, "they are NOT fish! They're mammals."

Just then, Polo slammed into the side of the houseboat.

From the boat's roofless center section, Marco leaped high into the air and spotted Polo. CLICK! CLICK! CLICK! The two chattered furiously at each other.

Avery, Ella, and Cora beached their kayaks onto the sandy shore. They threw down their paddles and raced toward the old pier.

"Look!" Myrtle screamed. "What's that crazy dolphin doing? I think it's going to attack us!"

At that moment, the first man noticed the girls racing toward them.

"Get out of here, you kids!" he yelled. "WHOOOAAA!" He stumbled over a bucket and his feet flew out from under him.

The second man hoisted a mass of thick fishing net and tried to cast it over Polo. He lost his balance and tumbled into the water. "Hate this net!" he cried, as his arms and legs immediately became tangled in the web of smelly, slimy rope.

Myrtle started to throw her bucket at Polo, but caught a glimpse of Avery sprinting straight toward her.

Avery glared at the woman defiantly. Then, she saw something sparkle in the moonlight.

SCREECH! The old pickup truck rumbled up and bounced to a stop. Two more cars skidded up behind it. The man in the fishing vest and hat jumped out of the truck, leaving his motor running.

"STOP!!" screamed Avery. "Get away from our dolphins!"

136

23

WAIT A MINUTE

"Cora!" shouted Avery. "Call 911!"

Cora whipped out her cell phone just as sirens began to scream and two police cars screeched up.

"You've been catching dolphins!" Avery shouted at Myrtle and the two men. "We've seen your boat following the dolphins. You're hiding the dolphins here!"

Two police officers charged up to handcuff the thieves.

Avery turned to the man who had gotten out of the old truck. "He's probably in on this, too," she shouted to the policemen. "We've seen him hanging out around Dolphin Cove!"

The man pulled a badge from one of the pockets of his fishing vest.

"I'm Detective Ned Parker," he said to the girls. "I was asked by the Save the Dolphin Organization to find these **perpetrators**. They've been sneaking up and down the East Coast, capturing wild dolphins. Then, they sell them for a lot of money to some unsavory dolphin attractions."

Just then, Avery realized that Evan, Mimi, Papa, and Cora's grandma surrounded the kids.

"I'm sorry, Avery!" said Evan. "I got worried. I had to tell Mimi and Papa everything."

"And he will get extra chocolate chip cookies for that," said Mimi, drawing Evan close in a hug.

"BAA-BAAAM!" yelled Evan.

"I'm sorry, Mimi," said Avery. "I had to find Marco. We couldn't let these people get away with him. I just got obsessed with solving the mystery."

"Just like your cousin Christina does," Mimi said with a sigh.

At that moment, Avery realized one of the officers was about to handcuff Myrtle. "Please wait a minute, Officer!" said Avery. "That dolphin necklace you're wearing belongs to my cousin Christina," she boldly announced to Myrtle. "You found it on the beach at Palmetto Bluff!"

Myrtle's face twisted in anger. She yanked the necklace over her head and thrust it into Avery's hand. She glared at the man next to her. "And you said you bought it for me," she snarled. "Ha!"

The man, already handcuffed, hung his head and looked away.

"Avery, you found it!" exclaimed Ella.

Ella and the others huddled around Avery to see the dolphin necklace in the palm of her hand. Avery slipped it over her head. "It's safe now!" she said proudly.

"Absolutely!" said Mimi. "Christina will be thrilled!"

"YESSS!" yelled Evan. He slapped each of the girls' hands in a jubilant high-five.

"I think it's time for a group hug!" said Cora, spreading out her arms.

24

LANTERN LAUNCH

The kids, along with Ned Parker, Mimi, Papa, and Cora's grandma stood near the water's edge at Dolphin Cove. Stars twinkled overhead. Headlights from their cars cast a glow on the mangrove trees and provided just enough light to make out the shadowy figures of dolphins.

Marco, Polo, and all the other dolphins frolicked in the cove.

"I'm sorry I scared you when I left the signs around here," said Detective Parker. "I was trying to keep you away from here. I was afraid for your safety if the thieves showed up. Obviously, I underestimated the four of you!"

Avery handed the detective a small piece of lime green paper. "Is this yours?" she asked.

"Yes, that is mine," he replied. "I wondered where that went! I found it when I was sneaking around the *Dolphin Catcher*. I thought it might be the number of dolphins the thieves were going to steal in each location."

"Darn!" said Evan, stomping his foot. "I thought for sure that was a ball game score."

"Well, let's be grateful it wasn't a dolphin catching score, right, buddy?" Detective Parker said.

Evan grinned. "Yes, sir, you're right!"

RING! RING! It was Christina with a FaceTime call to Avery.

Christina's smiling face popped up on Avery's phone. "Mimi said you wanted to talk to me," she said. "What's up? You guys having fun in Florida?"

Avery slipped out Christina's necklace from inside her t-shirt. She held it up to the camera on her phone. "Just look at this!"

Christina gasped. "My dolphin necklace!" she cried. "Where did you find it?"

"Well, first," said Avery, "there were dolphins disappearing from Dolphin Cove. We were trying to figure out what was going on—"

"Wait!" interrupted Christina. "You were trying to solve a mystery? I should have known! Poor Mimi! What is she going to do with these mystery-solving granddaughters?!"

As if she had heard her name, Mimi called to the kids, "Let's send up the Wish Lanterns! Papa has everything ready."

"Gotta go, Christina!" said Avery, blowing a kiss to her cousin. "I'll send you some video. You'll like this!"

Cora and her grandma unfolded their bright yellow Wish Lantern. They stood facing each other, holding out the bottom corners.

Papa flicked on a long lighter. Then, he reached under the rectangular lantern and lit the small fuel block. The flame took hold and the paper sides of the lantern gently expanded. Cora and her grandma stepped carefully to the edge of Dolphin Cove, holding their lantern high.

"One, two, three!" said Cora. The two released their hold, and the yellow lantern gracefully rose into the air and floated out to sea.

"Did you make a wish?" cried Ella, clapping her hands. Cora's big brown eyes were bright as she nodded her curly head yes.

One by one, Mimi and Papa helped the kids send their lanterns into the nighttime sky.

"Lift off!" yelled Evan as he launched his sky-blue lantern.

"It's beautiful!" exclaimed Ella as her fuchsia lantern floated up to join the others.

"Here's to the 'Summer of the Dolphin'!" shouted Avery, letting go of her lavender lantern.

The group quietly watched the glowing lanterns float across the dark sky. Waves gently slapped the shore and palm trees lightly swished in the breeze. Finally, all the lanterns had burned out, or disappeared into the clouds.

"Well, what did you all wish for?" asked Mimi as they turned to go.

Avery, Ella, Evan, and Cora looked at each other and grinned. Then, they shouted in unison, "To swim with the dolphins—AGAIN!"

The End

DO YOU LIKE MYSTERIES?

You have the chance to solve them!
You can solve little mysteries,
like figuring out
how to do your homework and
why your dog always hides your shoes.

You can solve big mysteries, like how to
program a fun computer game,
protect an endangered animal,
find a new energy source,
INVENT A NEW WAY TO DO SOMETHING, explore
outer space, and more!

You may be surprised to find
that *science*, **technology**,
engineering, math, and even
HISTORY, literature, and
ART can help you solve all kinds of
"mysteries" you encounter.

So feed your curiosity, learn all you can, apply
your creativity, and **be a mystery-solver too!**

- Carole Marsh

**More about the Science, Technology,
Engineering, & Math in this book**

DIAGRAM OF A BOTTLENOSE DOLPHIN

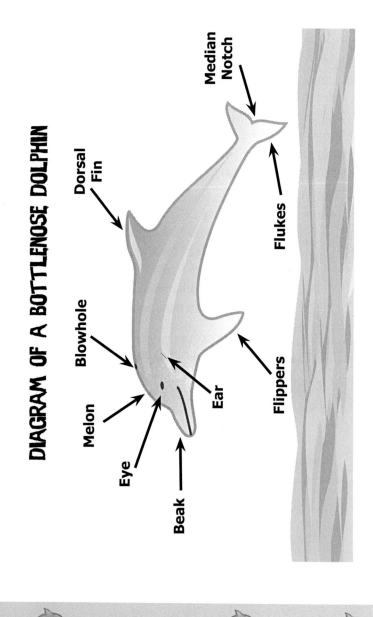

Melon

Blowhole

Dorsal Fin

Median Notch

Eye

Beak

Ear

Flippers

Flukes

DOLPHIN FACTS

- Dolphins are found in all of the oceans, but they tend to stay in areas with warmer temperatures.

- Dolphins are carnivores. That means they eat meat, like fish and squid.

- The bottlenose dolphin is the most common and well-known dolphin. Flipper, the famous dolphin featured in a 1960s TV show, was a bottlenose dolphin.

- The largest dolphin is the "killer whale," also known as orca.

- Female dolphins are called cows, males are called bulls, and young dolphins are called calves.

- Dolphins can stay underwater for about 15 minutes, but they cannot breathe underwater. They use a blowhole on top of their heads to breathe air when they come to the surface.

- Dolphins are well known for their sociable nature and high intelligence. They often swim very close to one another, and even rest fins on each other!

- Dolphins have a playful attitude. They jump out of the water, ride waves, play fight, and occasionally interact with humans swimming in the water. Scientists have even seen dolphins chase each other and toss seaweed back and forth!

- Dolphins have excellent eyesight and hearing, as well as the ability to use echolocation for navigation and hunting.

- Dolphins communicate with each other by using clicking, whistling, and other sounds.

PROBABILITY

Probability can be defined as *how likely it is that some event will happen.*

probability of an "event" = $\dfrac{\text{the number of ways the "event" can occur}}{\text{the total number of possible outcomes}}$

One of the best ways to understand probability is to use dice.

First, choose the "event." For example, if you want to know the probability of rolling a die and getting a "1" on top, that is the event.

Next, determine the total number of possible outcomes. Most dice have six sides, numbered 1-6. If you roll a die, there are six possible numbers that could appear on top: 1, 2, 3, 4, 5, 6. **The total number of possible outcomes is 6.**

Then, determine the number of ways the "event" can occur. **There is only one way you can get a "1" on top when you roll a die because there is only one "1" on the die.**

probability of rolling a 1 = $\dfrac{1}{6}$ *You can describe this as "one-out-of-six" or 17%.*

Pick a number from 1 to 6. What is the probability of a die landing on that particular number? **No matter what number you pick, the probability is 1/6!**

Now, what is the probability of rolling an even number? There are still 6 possible outcomes, so the bottom number is still 6. But this time, there are 3 possible ways the event could occur— if you roll a 2, 4, or 6. In this example, the top number is 3. **The probability of a die landing on an even number is 3/6, or 1/2. This can also be expressed as 50%.**

3D PRINTING

What is 3D printing? Many product designers and engineers are calling it "the next big thing!" 3D printing is a process that turns computer models into real things. A 3D printer can make virtually anything—from plastic

cups to plastic toys, stoneware vases, metal machine parts, and even jewelry!

The printer works by depositing thin layers of a material (like plastic) onto a surface. It then adds another layer, and another, and another, until the object is created. The final product is actually made of hundreds (or thousands) of tiny slices!

3D printers can use many different materials, like plastic, nylon, wax, or even steel. One type of 3D printer even uses strands of chocolate to make beautiful designs for delicious candies and gifts!

Most amazing of all, scientists are experimenting with **3D bioprinters** to create human body parts like bones, ears, and kidneys!

HOW DO DOLPHINS COMMUNICATE?

It is clear that dolphins communicate with each other! From birth, dolphins squawk, click, whistle, and squeak.

Each bottlenose dolphin identifies itself with a unique whistle. This whistle is so distinct that scientists can identify individual dolphins by examining their whistles on a sonogram (a visual image that shows sound).

Mama dolphins may whistle continuously to their calves for several days after birth. That way, the calves learn to identify their mothers. And by the time they are about one month of age, each calf has created its own signature whistle.

Dolphins also communicate nonverbally. Just as you gesture and change facial expressions as you talk, dolphins communicate through jaw claps, bubble blowing, rubbing fins together, and body movements, like tail slaps in the water!

ETYMOLOGY

The word **dolphin** comes from the Greek word **delphis** (dolphin), related to **delphys** (womb). Some experts say the name could come from the fact that dolphins bear live young. Therefore, **dolphin** could be interpreted as a "fish with a womb."

HOW THE SUN WARMS THE EARTH

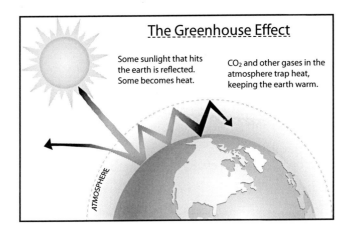

The Greenhouse Effect

Some sunlight that hits the earth is reflected. Some becomes heat.

CO_2 and other gases in the atmosphere trap heat, keeping the earth warm.

ATMOSPHERE

Have you ever heard of the "Greenhouse Effect"? It's a term used to describe how the Sun warms the Earth.

A greenhouse is a house with glass walls and a glass roof. People grow plants inside it because it stays warm year-round. Why? When sunlight shines in the greenhouse, it warms the air. The heat is trapped by the glass and can't escape, keeping the greenhouse toasty warm!

The Earth's atmosphere works in a similar way to a greenhouse. During the day, sunlight comes through the atmosphere and warms the surface of the Earth. The Earth's surface cools at night, releasing some of the heat back into the air. Gases in the atmosphere do what a greenhouse roof does, trapping some of that heat so it can't escape. That's what keeps our planet warm and livable!

GLOSSARY

anemone – invertebrate sea animal that looks like a flower and has clusters of brightly colored tentacles around the mouth

coincidence – two things that happen by accident, but seem to have some connection

commotion – noisy excitement or confusion

decomposing – slowly being destroyed and broken down by natural processes, chemicals, etc.

dejected – sad and depressed; being in low spirits

despicable – very bad or unpleasant

devoured – ate food hungrily or quickly

dilapidated – partly ruined or decayed, especially from age or lack of care

escorted – accompanied someone or something, usually for guidance or protection

estuary – body of water formed where freshwater from rivers and streams flows into the ocean, mixing with the seawater

foliage – the leaves of a plant or many plants

food chain – a succession of living organisms in which each serves as food for the next

gnarled – rough and twisted, especially with age

gravitational pull – the attraction that one object has for another object due to the invisible force of gravity

hoopla – excitement surrounding an event or situation

 incessantly – going on and on; not stopping or letting up

inspiration – someone or something that inspires, or influences, you to do something

 intriguing – arousing one's curiosity or interest; fascinating

Lowcountry – a geographic and cultural region located along South Carolina's coast

marsh – an area of soft, wet land usually overgrown by grasses and other plants

 perpetrator – someone who commits an illegal, evil, or criminal act

probability – how likely it is that some event will occur

 scrutinized – examined or inspected closely or thoroughly

shenanigans – funny or mischievous activity

 silhouette – a dark shape in front of a light background

spartina – a dense, fast-growing type of grass native to the Atlantic coast; also known as cordgrass

symbolism – the use of symbols to express or represent ideas or qualities in literature, art, etc.

 translucent – not transparent but clear enough to allow light to pass through

Enjoy this exciting excerpt from:

THE MYSTERY OF THE

TARANTULA TRAP

1

ARID-ZONA

Evan squinted his eyes into a tight, thin line. "Man, I'm roasting!" he said, cupping his hands above his eyes to shield them from the sun. His stick-straight blonde hair looked bleached white in the bright September afternoon.

"Ahh, the desert," Mimi said. She dabbed the sweat from her forehead with a scarlet handkerchief decorated with dainty white flowers. "Remind me again why we thought this was a good idea, Papa."

"Insects!" Papa boomed in his deep Southern drawl. "You said you had to see the desert insects. And just for the record, I never thought it was a good idea." Papa winked at Avery and Ella, who nodded in silent agreement.

Mimi and Papa had invited their grandchildren Avery, Ella, and Evan to travel with them to Tucson, Arizona, to explore a new city for a few days. Their baby sister Sadie stayed at home with their mom and dad. Mimi was a famous children's mystery writer, and often traveled across the globe to do research for her books.

This time, she wanted to visit the University of Arizona. She had spoken to a professor in the **entomology** department to help her learn about the local insects and

related creatures she wanted to include in her newest book. So Papa had loaded Mimi, the kids, and Mimi's giant red suitcase onto the *Mystery Girl* airplane and flew the crew all the way to Tucson.

On the flight in, Papa pointed out the steep, rocky mountain ridges that rimmed the desert valley below. In the valley sat a bustling city, with towering silver skyscrapers and jam-packed highways.

"This here is Tucson, Arizona!" he announced to the kids through the microphone attached to his pale green headset.

Once they landed at the airport, the kids were surprised at the desert environment around them.

"It's so flat here!" Ella said, scanning the scenery. Strands of shoulder-length blonde hair stuck to her upper lip like a mustache. Little beads of sweat built up on her forehead. "I guess those mountains fooled us!"

"And so hot!" Avery added. "But it feels dry, not sticky like at home." She pulled her long blonde hair off her neck and tied it into a ponytail.

"Now I know what a turkey feels like!" Evan said.

"What are you talking about?" Ella asked her little brother.

"You know, on Thanksgiving!" he said. "I feel like a turkey roasting in the oven!"

"The heat here is different from what we're used to," Mimi said. "In the southeastern part of the country, the summers feel like you're wrapped in a wet blanket with all that humidity. Here it's much drier—but still hot, all right!"

"The first thing we need to do is get acquainted with the land," Papa said. He tucked his white cowboy hat on his head and ushered Mimi and the kids to the rental car waiting by the airplane hangar. Papa had specially requested a jeep with huge off-road tires, big metal roll bars on the roof, and spotlights for exploring at night. Its shiny red paint gleamed in the bright sun.

"So how do you like our ride?" he asked Mimi.

She smiled and kissed his cheek. "You know it's my favorite color! And as long as it has air conditioning, I'm good to go!"

"It's awesome!" Evan exclaimed.

"You'll soon see lots of things are a bit different out here in the Wild West," Papa announced.

Mimi and Papa lived in Palmetto Bluffs, South Carolina, where the landscape was lush and old oak trees dripped with Spanish moss. Their Lowcountry home was close to the Atlantic Ocean—a far cry from the landlocked city of Tucson.

"I love how you can see for miles and miles here," Avery observed.

"Just wait until you see the sunsets," Mimi said. "They are magnificent!"

Papa laughed. "Like Dorothy said in *The Wizard of Oz*, we're not in 'South Carolina' anymore!"